The Listener

Elizabeth Laird

Illustrated by Pauline Hazelwood

A & C Black · London

For Barny, George, Polly,
Sally and Fred

Chapter One

It was Friday afternoon and school was over for another week. Gavin Foster should have been in a great mood.

But he wasn't.
He was depressed.
He was fed up.
And he was furious with his mum.

Just because you're going away for the weekend, I don't see why I've got to go away too. I could have stayed here on my own, easily, or gone to one of my mates.

6

Gavin walked down to the bus stop. A crowd of his friends was standing outside the fish and chip shop.

The bus came. Gavin climbed on board and sat hunched at the back, hardly bothering to look out of the window.

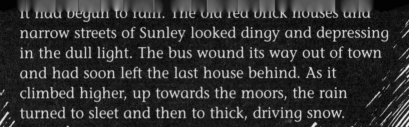

It had begun to rain. The old red brick houses and narrow streets of Sunley looked dingy and depressing in the dull light. The bus wound its way out of town and had soon left the last house behind. As it climbed higher, up towards the moors, the rain turned to sleet and then to thick, driving snow.

That's all I need. I'll be snowed in, and have to stay up here for weeks and weeks. Just my luck!

The bus turned the last sharp corner before the top of the hill. Gavin picked up his bag and pushed his way to the front.

Chapter Two

The biting wind, laden with snow, stung his cheeks. Gavin zipped up his jacket and began to trudge down the path that led across the open moor towards Mrs Foster's lonely cottage. He shivered, and started to walk faster. He could see a light in the window now and he knew his gran would have cooked a great supper for him.

Gavin was nearly at the cottage door when he almost tripped over something. He looked down.

The telephone wire's collapsed! The weight of snow must have brought it down.

Bad luck, Mum! I won't be able to phone you after all.

Gran! Are you there?

He knocked on the front door, but Mrs Foster didn't open it at once, like she usually did.

No one answered.

15

Gavin looked round the warm, cosy little room. The fire was lit and still burning brightly. The table was set for two people and he could smell a delicious meaty smell coming from the tiny kitchen. One of Gran's casseroles was cooking in the oven.

Suddenly, he ducked in terror as a black and white streak shot past his head.

Mrs Foster's tame magpie settled on the table and strutted up and down, looking nervously at Gavin. The kerfuffle had disturbed something else, too. A rustling, scrabbling noise came from a box near the fire.

Gavin went over to look. Two small black eyes peered up at him from inside a halo of prickles.

He ran upstairs
and looked quickly
into the two tiny
bedrooms.

Are you there,
Gran?

Nobody answered.

He went to the front door and stepped out again,
into the driving wind.

She must be
outside somewhere.

19

It had stopped snowing and the clouds were beginning to clear away but the daylight was going fast now and the snow-covered moors looked strange and eerie. Gavin kept his head down, his eyes on the footprints.

Suddenly, he stopped. The snow was trampled and messed up here, as if there'd been some kind of struggle.

Leading away from the beaten snow were several sets of prints, the ones he'd been following already, some tiny paw-marks that could have been a cat's, and some larger prints, like those of a dog or a fox. And in the snow, bright as poppy petals, were drops of brilliant scarlet. Gavin knelt down to look at them.

Chapter Three

He looked round. The human footprints went on towards the wood, but they had changed. They were more spaced out now, as though the person had been trying to run. The moors Gavin thought he knew so well looked suddenly menacing in the fading light.

He felt his heart begin to thump uncomfortably hard inside his chest. He looked uneasily over his shoulder and ran on into the wood. It was much darker now and he could hardly see the trail of footprints which seemed to be meandering, as if the person had become puzzled or confused.

Twigs seemed to reach out and touch him and shivers of fear ran down his spine. All of a sudden he trod on a rotten branch which was lying just under the snow. It broke with a loud crack. Gavin nearly jumped out of his skin, but he steadied himself and went on.

Then he heard a noise. He stopped to listen. There it was again. Someone was groaning not far away! His skin prickled with fright as he tiptoed cautiously towards the noise.

Then he saw it, a long dark shape under the trees. Someone was lying in the snow.

Gran!

He ran up and sank down on to his knees beside the still figure. Even in the darkness he recognised her.

Gran! What's happened? Are you hurt? Did someone attack you? Say something, Gran!

The old woman opened her eyes.

Gavin! Oh, thank *goodness* you've come. It's my leg. I think - I'm sure it's broken.

Gavin tore off his jacket and tucked it round her, then he took off as fast as he could through the trees.

He knew the cottage. It had been empty when he'd been here as a little kid and he'd often played round it. He hadn't been there since it had been done up and the new people had moved in.

The cottage was much grander than he remembered. An extension had been built on one side and there was a fence all round it. Gavin opened the gate and went up to the front door. He rang the bell.

Chapter Four

The door opened at once. A woman stood there. She was big, blonde and angry. Behind her, Gavin caught sight of a darker, young girl who was watching him with an intent expression on her face.

31

As the window slammed shut again, Gavin felt some-body tapping him on the shoulder. He turned round.

The dark girl he had glimpsed inside the house was standing behind him. She stood looking at him, a puzzled expression on her face.

Listen!
You've got to listen!
She's cold. She'll die of cold
if I don't get help soon.

The girl shook her head, then took hold of Gavin's arm and turned him round so that his face was lit by the beam of the lamp above the front door.

What the matter?

Her voice sounded as if it came from the back of her throat. Gavin could hardly understand her.

My gran. I told you. Are you deaf, or what?

She nodded vigorously.

Yes. Deaf. I'm deaf. Tell me again. I can read your lips.

Gavin described the place as well as he could. The operator's questions seemed to go on for ever.

Please hurry. She's so cold. I'm afraid...

Don't worry. We'll get someone out to you as soon as possible. It sounds like one for the air ambulance. Don't move her. Just cover her with plenty of blankets.

Chapter Five

It was quite dark by now. The only light came from
the unearthly white radiance of the snow. Out in
the open, Gavin could follow the trail of his own
footprints quite easily, but it was difficult once they
were among the trees. He had to go slowly, peering
down at the ground to find his way.

Suddenly, he realized he was lost.

But the girl had seen him stop and look round and she called out,

Use the torch!

With a shudder of relief, he remembered he was carrying it and switched it on. There were his footprints, only a few metres away. He ran along them and there, a little further on, he saw the long, dark shape of his grandmother. She was lying horribly still in the snow.

Gran!

The girl knelt down beside Gavin. Gently, she lifted the old woman's head and Gavin, seeing what she was doing, took the pillow and tucked it into place. Then she began to wrap the blankets round the old lady.

You're shivering. You'd better put your jacket on again. She's got the blankets now.

Gavin lifted the jacket, which was still covering his gran's chest. A black shape uncurled itself and streaked off across the snow with a terrified yowl. Gavin and the girl started back with fright.

Gavin laughed shakily.

Don't worry, Gran. We'll go after her in a minute. Let's get you comfortable first.

He wrapped the blankets round her, tucking them underneath as far as he dared, though she groaned with pain whenever he touched her leg.

48

Mrs Foster murmured something. She spoke too quietly for Gavin to hear, but the girl seemed to understand what she wanted to say even though it was too dark for her to read the old woman's lips.

50

Chapter Six

Shelley was holding Mrs Foster's hands, rubbing them between her own. She had heard nothing.

Gavin touched her arm and pointed to the lights above. Then he shone the torch on to his lips.

They're coming. It's the helicopter ambulance. Stay here with Gran. I'll go and show them the way here.

Shelley nodded. Gavin took off like a hare, bounding through the wood towards the open moor.
The helicopter was almost overhead when he ran out from under the trees. He jumped up and down, waving his arms like a madman.

The great machine slowly settled on the frozen moor, the wind from its propellers churning the snow up in a wild white storm. The door slid back and three people jumped out.

Over here! This way!

They pulled a stretcher and some bags of medical equipment out of the helicopter.

Don't go so fast, lad.

The oldest ambulance man panted as he followed Gavin into the wood.

Keep that torch still, will you? No point in all of us crashing into the trees and breaking our legs.

A few minutes later, they had reached
Mrs Foster, and in what seemed like no
time at all, she had been tucked on to the
stretcher and the ambulance crew were
gently sliding it into the helicopter.

The old lady had kept her eyes shut, wincing with pain whenever she moved, but just as the pilot was about to close the door, she opened them wide and looked at Gavin.

Gavin nodded, then the pilot shut the door, the helicopter's huge propellers began to whirl round and round, and the gleaming machine lifted itself effortlessly into the air.

Chapter Seven

Gavin stood for a long time, watching until the helicopter's lights had disappeared over the horizon towards the glow of light from the city below.

What do I do now?

He didn't like the idea of staying in Gran's cottage all on his own, but he had no choice. He looked round. Shelley had disappeared.

I suppose she's gone home. Back to Johnny Mason and that awful woman.

He thrust his hands deep into his pockets, hunched his shoulders and walked back towards the cottage.

As he pushed the door open, a smell of burnt food hit him right in the nose.

Oh no! The casserole!

He ran into the kitchen, turned off the oven and pulled out the big dish inside it. The top of the stew was blackened, but underneath it looked fine. Appetizing, in fact.

Gavin suddenly realized he was hungry. He was still cold, too. He put some wood on the fire and fanned it to a blaze then he fetched a plate and a fork and put them on the table.

At least I won't starve.

He was just about to help himself to some of the casserole when he heard a sound outside the front door.

Is anyone there?

No one answered.

The door opened. Shelley came in, and in her arms was a big black cat.

Tinker struggled out of Shelley's arms and walked stiffly towards the fire. She lay down and began to lick at the dark blood that had congealed along her flank.

Gavin turned Shelley to look at him.

Is she badly hurt?

She bent over the cat and gently stroked the matted fur away from the ugly looking gash. Tinker snarled at her and pushed out her claws, but to Gavin's surprise she didn't try to scratch Shelley or leap away from her touch.

Not bad. Best thing is to let her rest. She'll lick the wound clean. Give her something to eat.

68

Chapter Eight

A sudden loud knock on the door made Gavin jump.

BANG BANG

Who on earth..? Perhaps it's someone with news about Gran?

Nervously, he opened the door.
Into the room stepped Johnny Mason.

Is Mrs Foster all right?

And is my sister here?

Before Gavin could answer, Shelley flew past him and Gavin watched with amazement as she began flicking her hands and fingers about in a tirade of complicated gestures.

There was more frantic
signing from Shelley.

73

Shelley laughed and clapped her hands. Then she signed something to Johnny.

I don't see why not.

What's she saying?

Gavin was beginning to wish he could do sign language too. It looked cool.

74

Gavin shook his head in disbelief. Then he caught
Johnny's eye. They both laughed.

Gavin put another plate on
the table and began to dish
out the casserole.